The
THREE GIFTS

The THREE GIFTS

PATRICIA COOK ORR

illustrations by WILSON ONG

DESERET
BOOK

Salt Lake City, Utah

Pages 38 and 39: "Joy to the World"; text by Isaac Watts, altered by William W. Phelps. *Hymns of The Church of Jesus Christ of Latter-day Saints* (Salt Lake City: The Church of Jesus Christ of Latter-day Saints, 1985), no. 201.

Visit us at DeseretBook.com

Library of Congress Cataloging-in-Publication Data
Orr, Patricia Cook.
    The three gifts / Patricia Cook Orr ; illustrations by Wilson Ong.
        p. cm.
    Summary: Christmas story about Mary, Joseph, and Jesus, and what happened to the gifts of the Three Kings.
    Includes bibliographical references.
    ISBN 978-1-60641-847-5 (alk. paper)
    1. Jesus Christ—Nativity—Fiction. 2. Magi—Fiction. 3. Christmas stories. I. Ong, Wilson J. II. Title.
PS3615.R5885T47 2010
813'.6—dc22   2010019687

Printed in the United States of America   10/2010
Publishers Printing, Salt Lake City, UT

10 9 8 7 6 5 4 3 2 1

To my mom,
for her beautiful life
of selfless giving.

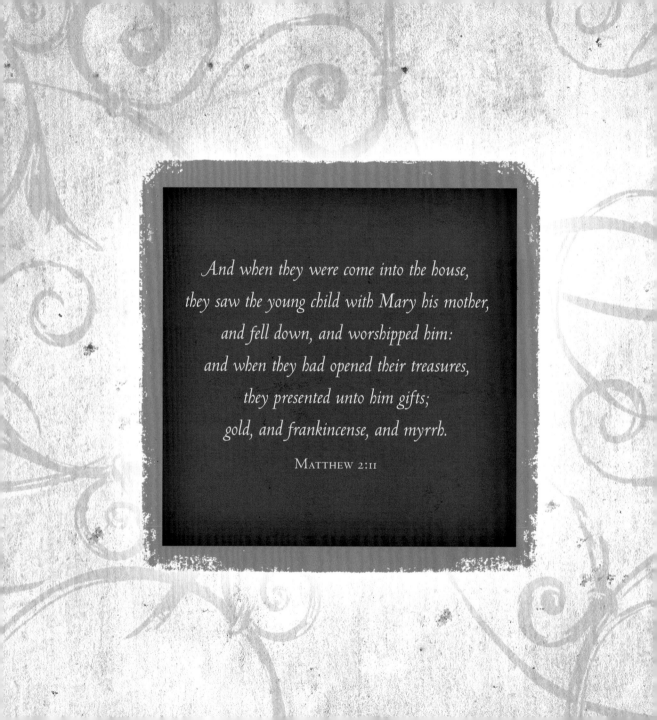

And when they were come into the house,
they saw the young child with Mary his mother,
and fell down, and worshipped him:
and when they had opened their treasures,
they presented unto him gifts;
gold, and frankincense, and myrrh.

MATTHEW 2:11

Mary gazed in wide-eyed amazement at the three opulent gifts set before her. Separately, each one possessed remarkable beauty. Together they graced her simple home with their exquisite splendor. Yet they were not hers.

On this quiet evening while Joseph was away, travelers had reached her door. The unexpected visitors had startled Mary, but their appearance was even more perplexing. Their leathery skin was wrinkled as much from sun as from age. Long, wiry whiskers lay stiffly against regal robes denoting nobility. And in their faces Mary found childlike anticipation.

She felt moved to invite them in.

As the wealthy kings entered the small, sparsely furnished room, Mary felt lowly. She had very little to offer these guests. While the men were seating themselves, Mary brought out a few figs to share, which they graciously accepted. They began telling their story, and Mary understood. Led by a star, they had traveled a great distance for a single purpose: to see her son.

The young mother crossed the room, bent over a small cradle, and lifted Jesus from his tiny bed. As the Wise Men produced their lavish treasures, Mary sat awestruck, holding her son. No one seemed certain what to say next.

A sweet lull settled over the room. It was neither heavy nor awkward, so in the silence Mary studied the three gifts. The first was a large wooden box heaped with gold that glimmered in the lamplight. Carved into its skillfully crafted lid was an exotic landscape framed with inlaid mother-of-pearl. Mary could hardly wait for Joseph to return. He would appreciate its masterful carpentry.

Next to it stood a rotund porcelain canister glazed a deep sapphire blue and filled with fragrant frankincense. The room's rough-hewn furnishings appeared coarse when mirrored in its flawless finish. The mounded lid rested next to it on the small table, allowing the frankincense resin to release its sweet savor. Mary felt certain that when it burned, this frankincense would produce smoke that would be particularly white.

Lamplight flickered through the third gift's translucent surface, revealing the pure myrrh oil the vessel held. Made of white alabaster, its long, narrow neck paralleled the delicate handle before curving gracefully outward to form the belly. A slight breeze lifted the spicy aromas and mingled them together, perfuming the room with their natural incense.

It was then that Mary felt the weight of an overwhelming responsibility settle into her heart. These exquisite gifts, so freely given, could not be received lightly. She and Joseph must use them well. Still cradling her young son, Mary turned to face the Wise Men with tears welling in her eyes. She could not conjure words to adequately thank them for their generosity.

But where words failed, her actions became clear and purposeful. Mary moved forward to place her precious child into the arms of the nearest Wise Man. His expressive eyes betrayed his uncertainty. Still she persisted and tenderly adjusted his awkwardly outstretched arm to receive the baby. Then she nestled the small body into his thick, travel-worn hands.

Any pretense vanished, and he brought the tiny child close to his heart. Then, sensing the end of his long journey, he bowed his head the way the sun descends in the evening sky as it surrenders to the peaceful night. Warm tears crept down his wrinkled, whiskered cheek as it rested on the soft crown of the young king. Time stood still, yielding its steady march to the reverence of this moment.

The King of Kings was cradled by a king.

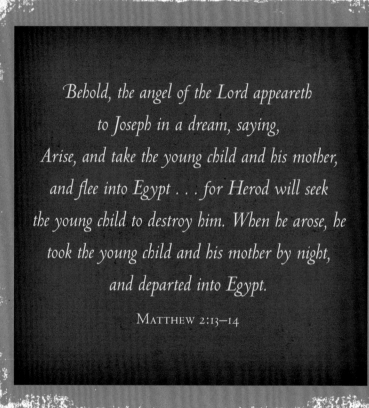

*Behold, the angel of the Lord appeareth
to Joseph in a dream, saying,
Arise, and take the young child and his mother,
and flee into Egypt . . . for Herod will seek
the young child to destroy him. When he arose, he
took the young child and his mother by night,
and departed into Egypt.*

MATTHEW 2:13–14

Nervous tension loomed in the night air as Joseph and Mary traveled quietly toward Egypt. The rhythmic pull of the donkey's stride tilted their cart to and fro, rocking little Jesus to sleep as He lay hidden between them.

At the crest of a small hill, drunken men set upon them like demons from the darkness. They wore the uniform of Herod's ruthless guards. Mary instinctively put her hand on her sleeping son and looked up at her husband in a silent plea.

Above Joseph's objections, the filthy thieves rummaged through the cart's scant baggage. Muttering and cursing, they slashed their daggers across the bound belongings and then disgustedly tossed the contents out onto the roadside. Some landed with heavy thuds on the hard-packed ground. Others fluttered like autumn leaves. One crash rang out with the familiar sounds of iron scraping on wood, announcing that Joseph's carpentry tools had been thrown aside. But Mary took courage, and she hurriedly draped her cloak over the three precious gifts near her feet.

The leader of the guards staggered along the side of the cart and came toward Mary. His breath smelled of intoxicating indulgence. Attempting to board the cart, he stumbled into her. Mary screamed. The commotion startled Jesus, who began to cry.

Upon hearing the child's voice, the guards resolved to carry out Herod's orders for babies in that region. The men lunged toward Jesus, intent on murder. Mary threw herself over her son, and Joseph dove to protect them both against the reaching arms of the wicked fiends.

Then Joseph's mind lit upon an inspired plan. He reached down and pulled a heavy object into his grasp. He called out in a loud voice as he hefted a large rectangular box over his head. Inlaid mother-of-pearl glistened briefly in the starlight before Joseph hurled it out into the darkness. Its beautiful carving shattered upon impact, causing golden treasure to spill out onto the rocky desert road. Herod's thugs immediately gave up their deadly intention and ran toward the pile, each greedily claiming a portion of the spoils.

In the blitz of confusion, Joseph hurried the donkey forward while an argument ensued behind them among the covetous men. As they distanced themselves from the thieves, Mary picked up her son and held Him close. She tried to calm Him but found that holding Him brought comfort to her. She leaned her head against Joseph's shoulder and exhaled.

The danger was past, and one gift was used. On that night, the Wise Men's endowment served a noble purpose. The gold from a king had ransomed the life of the small boy who would one day ransom all men from death.

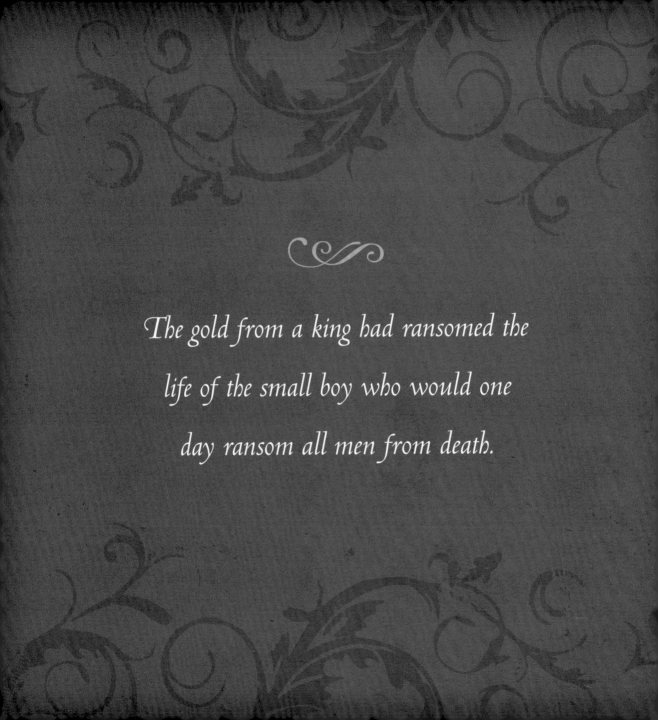

The gold from a king had ransomed the life of the small boy who would one day ransom all men from death.

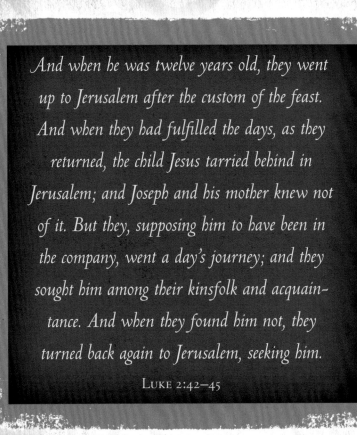

And when he was twelve years old, they went up to Jerusalem after the custom of the feast. And when they had fulfilled the days, as they returned, the child Jesus tarried behind in Jerusalem; and Joseph and his mother knew not of it. But they, supposing him to have been in the company, went a day's journey; and they sought him among their kinsfolk and acquaintance. And when they found him not, they turned back again to Jerusalem, seeking him.

Luke 2:42–45

Joseph and Mary stood together on the temple balcony trying to recognize Jesus among the thousands of worshipers below. For three days they had combed Jerusalem's crowded streets searching for Him.

Hope drove their desperate quest, but today discouragement was giving way to despair. Alone in Jerusalem, Jesus could fall victim to the wiles of any number of evil men.

An engulfing guilt pressed on Mary for allowing herself to believe that Jesus was in their traveling company without personally seeing to it. She yearned for her lost son.

This year marked Jesus' first experience with temple rites, so His mother had insisted on bringing the pure frankincense. Symbolic of holy authority, it seemed fitting to burn some with their Passover lamb. Knowing its value, Joseph thought it was safest in his possession. He had carried it in a large satchel all the way from Nazareth.

On the balcony, Joseph removed the satchel from his shoulder to rest a moment from its load. Looking down at the swirling masses, he leaned against the banister and slowly shifted his weight from one foot to the other. He was tired in a way that was deeper than physical exhaustion. Mary's heart went out to him.

Joseph lifted the bag on to his other shoulder and led Mary down the shaded breezeway. A peculiar group drew their attention; several priests huddled outside a small room. Nearing the entrance, Mary heard a distinct adolescent voice. She pressed past Joseph and entered the room headlong.

There sat Jesus calmly in the center! Acting on instinct, she strode to Him, wrapped Him in her arms, and exclaimed, "Son, why hast thou thus dealt with us?" The words tumbled out of her in an avalanche of exasperated emotions and bounced awkwardly around the room before finally echoing back into her own ears. All other conversations ceased. Even amid her joy, Mary's heart sank into the pit of her stomach. Having forgotten herself, she could not retract her words.

In the silence, Mary glanced around at the room's occupants. It was filled with esteemed scholars, doctors, temple priests, and even the high priest in his breastplate and elaborate robes. She was embarrassed at her outburst.

"Wist ye not that I must be about my Father's business?" came her son's steady response. Hushed mutterings passed throughout the elders.

Seeing her distress, one young priest with auburn hair came to Mary's aid. Speaking from the perspective of a confident youth, he quipped, "The son was never lost, but his parents were!" He finished with a flourish, shifting the room's focus away from Mary. Once boys themselves, the circle of men laughed warmly in benevolent understanding.

Gratitude replaced anxiety. Still, Mary's emotions left her unsteady. She and Joseph had heard a message in Jesus' reply that the priests had not. They had been reminded that Jesus was divine. Knowing the secret kept by the holy family, Mary looked down as the elders exited past her.

She felt Joseph step forward to her side. The young priest with the auburn hair paused in front of Mary as he left the room. With emphasis on each word, he reassured her, "Jesus is an honorable son." When he spoke, she looked up and met his gaze. Her demeanor softened as she looked into his kind eyes. "Yes," she answered in a hoarse whisper, "yes, he is."

As the high priest approached them, Joseph removed the satchel from his shoulder once again. This time he did not place it on his other shoulder as expected. Instead he knelt down, opened the bag, and removed the beautiful porcelain canister. In a gesture of honor to the boy's true Father, Joseph held out the jar as an offering to the high priest. Mary bowed her head in consent.

Without understanding the symbolic moment, the high priest accepted the token of gratitude out of Joseph's hands and into his own. Indeed, Jesus did know His place. And His parents did too.

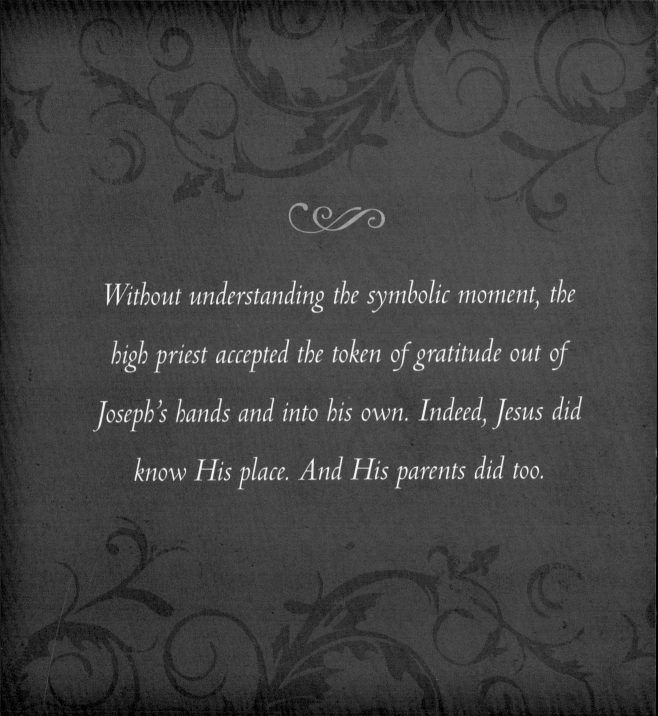

Without understanding the symbolic moment, the high priest accepted the token of gratitude out of Joseph's hands and into his own. Indeed, Jesus did know His place. And His parents did too.

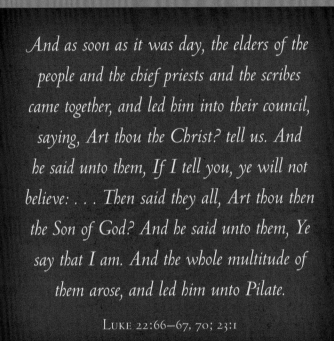

And as soon as it was day, the elders of the people and the chief priests and the scribes came together, and led him into their council, saying, Art thou the Christ? tell us. And he said unto them, If I tell you, ye will not believe: . . . Then said they all, Art thou then the Son of God? And he said unto them, Ye say that I am. And the whole multitude of them arose, and led him unto Pilate.

LUKE 22:66–67, 70; 23:1

This Passover morning, Mary traversed the crowd in blind denial of the events unfolding around her. The heated mob pushed on her from all sides while they awaited Pilate's return, hissing their relentless rebuke toward her son Jesus. Her head spun with the sounds of the seething crowd. She gathered her veil against the rising heat and mounting contempt.

Several temple priests moved independently through the crowd. Once Jesus had been safe in their company. Perhaps she could find a sympathetic priest to whom she could plead for His release. Then she saw him.

A certain chief priest moved assertively through the frenzied gathering. More than twenty years had passed, but Mary recognized his auburn hair now flecked with gray. Certainly he would remember her. Though they had met only once, she had regarded him fondly all these years and felt a certain kinship with him because of the kindness he had shown to her in an awkward moment. He had seen her need then; surely he would help now. Holding a position of such respect, he could be the one to calm this mob. She determined to reach him.

Jesus appeared on the balcony above the crowd, bound and bleeding behind Pilate. The horde continued their verbal attack. Their rumblings grew until they erupted with vindictive bursts of self-righteous arrogance, "Crucify him! Crucify him!"

It felt to Mary as though their vicious cries would consume her, but still she sought a way to rescue her son. Calling upon her inner strengths, Mary made her way through the crowd. Finally she came near the chief priest with the auburn hair. He had stopped to watch Pilate on the balcony. She came close behind him, leaned forward, and reached out to him, ready to plead her cause. At that moment Pilate called out, "Behold your King."

As Mary's hand landed on the priest's upper arm, his opposite hand immediately grabbed her wrist, and he spun around. She stepped forward to keep her balance, and the gap between them closed. Now face to face, he took her in a firm grip. Those eyes, once soft and laughing, now blazed wildly with savage anticipation. His mouth was already forming his next words. "Crucify him!" he shouted into her face. His spittle stuck in her veil.

The man to whom she had once been so grateful saw her only as one more person he could stir into the frenzy. He pushed his vile frame past her in bloodthirsty fervor, and Mary nearly fainted. There was no hope! These priests, moving separately through the mob, fueled its ravenous anger. They urged the fury and led the wicked cry! Once, Jesus sat safely in their company. Today, they stood united as His greatest threat.

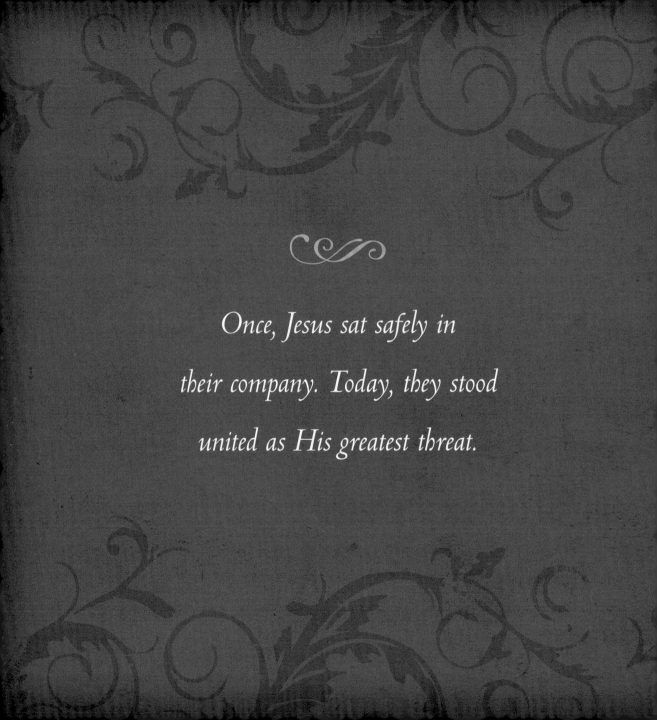

Once, Jesus sat safely in
their company. Today, they stood
united as His greatest threat.

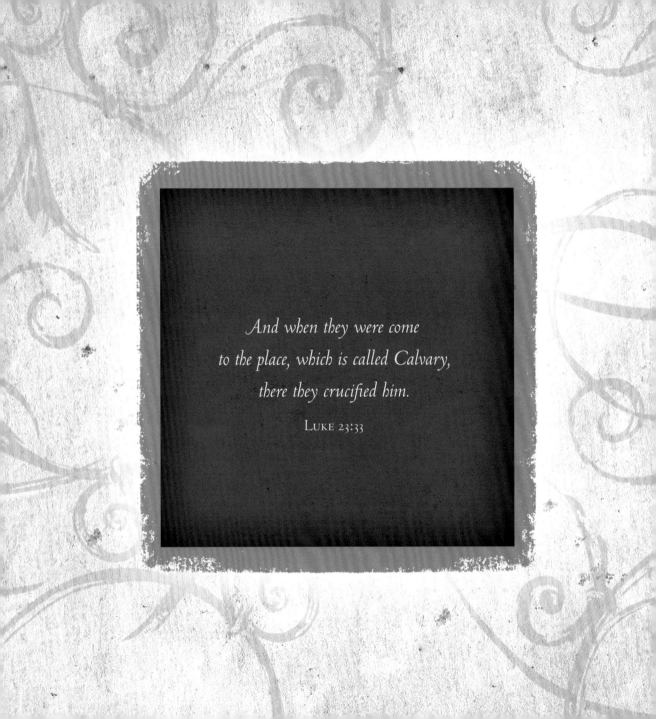

*And when they were come
to the place, which is called Calvary,
there they crucified him.*

LUKE 23:33

Mary witnessed another drop of blood fall to the dusty earth. Kneeling at Jesus' feet, she saw how they quivered from pain. She was powerless to relieve His suffering; she couldn't even touch Him. Never had she known such intense anguish. Her unrestrained tears streamed off her cheeks and onto the ground, where they mixed with His blood. Her body shuddered rhythmically to her sobs. Defeated, she remained there upon the ground, aware of nothing beyond herself and her son. Her eyes closed.

Metallic pieces hit against each other. Deep voices argued from afar.

These sounds mingled with her distant memories, and she drifted back thirty-three years.

She was young again and holding her small son safely to her bosom. Joseph sat beside her, intent on driving the donkey forward. Behind them, Herod's guards greedily picked their spoils out of the twisted, broken box that had been a precious gift to her son. Covetous voices argued over those gold pieces just as they now fought for His raiment. Mary was yanked back to the present. Roman soldiers bickered as they cast lots for His coat.

Nothing would spare His life today. This ransom was not to be paid with gold.

"Please, dear Father," she prayed, "let it be done."

A familiar voice began speaking. It was gentle yet resolute in its instruction. Each word brought Mary out of the deep reaches within herself. Her attention came into focus as she heard the familiar word, "Mother." She was ready to listen. "Woman, behold thy son."

Reluctantly, obediently, Mary looked up into the face of her dying son. From the cross He looked down on her with compassion. It was time to say good-bye. For a moment there was only He and she.

Looking into each other's eyes, they said farewell without speaking. A brief smile crossed Jesus' lips; then, with His eyes He redirected her attention to John. She felt John tenderly lift her and allowed herself to be led away.

From the cross He looked down on

her with compassion. It was time to say

good-bye. For a moment there was only

He and she. Looking into each other's eyes,

they said farewell without speaking.

And from that hour that disciple

took her unto his own home.

John 19:27

Inside the city walls once more, Mary raised her head in an attempt to get her bearings. It was still the Passover. John pointed in the direction of the temple, where the white smoke of frankincense rose to heaven. It seemed to Mary that the smoke burned particularly white.

She forced herself to focus on John's face and made one request. In response, John changed their course and walked her to a small dwelling. There, in the stillness of the filtered light, she reached into an old wooden chest. Her hands trembled as she took out a carefully wrapped package. John watched her caress it in her lap as she removed the covering to reveal a slender, aged pitcher of white alabaster. The translucent vessel was illuminated in the sunbeams coming through a small window. Mary uncorked the jar allowing the myrrh's musky aroma to fill her senses.

As she ran her fingers slowly across its surface, memories crowded Mary's mind. Once more she saw the travel-worn Wise Men dressed in regal robes sitting in her home long ago. They watched her as she gently placed her child into one Wise Man's uncertain hands. She felt anew the king's relief at the end of his journey when his whiskered cheek rested against the crown of her son's head. Tears traced their familiar lines down her cheeks.

Now again, her actions were purposeful. She pressed the vessel into John's hands. "Please," she whispered, "use this myrrh to anoint His head. Let it seep into the wounds left by the thorns. It is a king's gift. Let this be His crown."

John took the pitcher from her and escorted Mary to his home, where he saw to her every comfort. Leaving to fulfill her charge, he turned around at the door to look on her once more. She bore an expression of tranquility, as though her efforts had been accepted, her stewardship completed, and she knew it.

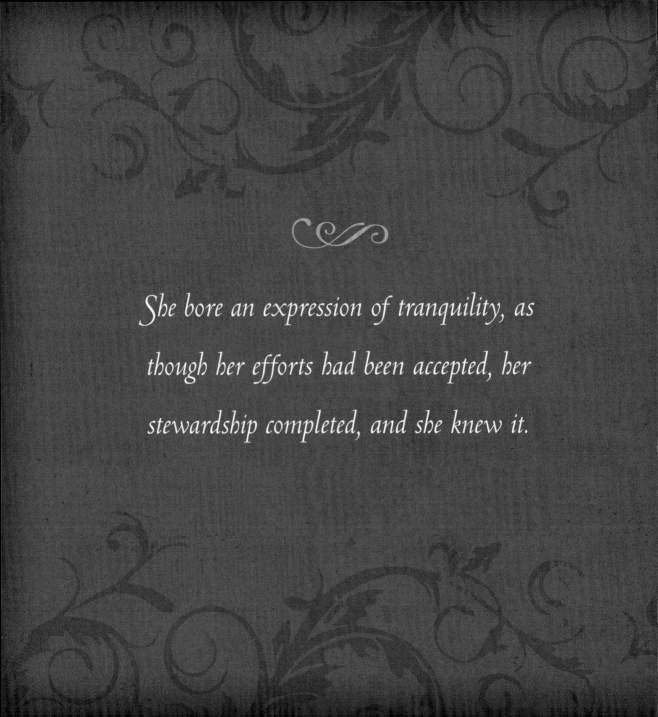

She bore an expression of tranquility, as though her efforts had been accepted, her stewardship completed, and she knew it.

Let ev'ry heart prepare him room.

"Joy to the World"

The three gifts brought by the Wise Men were used well: gold ransomed Jesus' life, frankincense gave testimony of His divinity, and myrrh confirmed His atoning sacrifice. Yet the three gifts He offers to us are infinitely more precious:

He ransoms all men from death.

A Divine Being, He lived on Earth as our Exemplar.

He completed the Atonement and extends grace to all who choose to receive it.

These gifts He offers to us freely today and forevermore.

So let us join our praise with that of heaven and the angels. "Joy to the world, the Lord is come. Let earth receive her King."

About the Author

PATRICIA COOK ORR was raised in Lake Shore, Utah. She served an LDS mission in Frankfurt, Germany, and later graduated from Brigham Young University in humanities. She and her husband, Eric, reside in Laie, Hawaii, with their six children. A first-time author, Patricia wrote *The Three Gifts* as a Christmas gift to her mother.

About the Illustrator

WILSON JAY ONG grew up in the San Francisco Bay Area and received his BFA from Brigham Young University. In addition to being a professional artist and illustrator since 1983, Wilson has taught art, presented workshops, and exhibited his work in a variety of venues. He and his family currently live in Corning, New York.